BEDTIME FOR BABY SLOTH

DANIELLE MCLEAN

SARAH WARD

LiTTLE TiGER

LONDON

High up in the treetops Mummy Sloth called to her baby, "Time for bed, little one!"

But Baby Sloth wasn't ready for bed. She was having too much fun!

"Mummy," she laughed, "I can't go to bed yet.
I haven't said goodnight to the stars and
the moon."

Mummy Sloth smiled. "How could I forget!
OK, you say your goodnights. But then
it's bedtime. Little sloths need their rest."

Together the sloths looked up at the shimmering sky.
"Goodnight moon," beamed Baby Sloth.
"Goodnight stars," added Mummy.
"Now come on, little one, it's time to snuggle up."

"But Mummy, we can't go to sleep yet. We haven't sung to the birds. They need their lullaby, otherwise THEY won't be able to sleep," explained Baby Sloth.

"Well, we can't have that!" replied Mummy Sloth, laughing.

So Mummy and Baby cuddled up together and hummed soft lullabies to the birds as they swooped through the sky.

All was quiet and still when suddenly Baby Sloth's
belly gave a gurgle and grumble.
     "Mummy, I think I need a bedtime snack," she giggled.

"Just one piece of fruit," answered Mummy Sloth,
leaning back so Baby could pick a juicy one.
"The sun is rising and that means bed for baby sloths!"

But Baby STILL wasn't ready to sleep!
She was too busy hanging from
her favourite branch.

"Oh dear me! What can we do to settle
you down?" asked Mummy Sloth.
"How about a bedtime story?"

"Oh yes!" smiled Baby Sloth,
climbing over to her mummy.

While Mummy told Baby's favourite bedtime story, Baby cuddled up on top of her belly and gave a big, stretchy yawn.

"You're the best at telling stories," sighed Baby Sloth.

And just as Mummy was reaching the end, Baby whispered, "Mummy, I think I'm ready to . . ."

"Rest?" finished Mummy,
with a kiss on her nose.

Baby Sloth was finally
starting to snooze.

ZZZZZ

As the sun rose above the horizon, Mummy Sloth
wished Baby Sloth the sweetest of dreams.

"Sleep tight, sleepyhead," she sighed.
And the two sloths dozed happily, all day long.